Praise For
SIR SIMON: SUPER SCARER

Winner of the 2020 Chocolate Lily Award

Winner of the 2019 Shining Willow Award

Shortlisted for the 2019 Christie Harris Illustrated Children's Literature Prize

One of CCBC'S Best Books for Kids & Teens, Spring 2019

D0317893

CALE ATKINSON is an illustrator, writer and animator living
lakeside with his family in Kelowna, British Columbia, whose books
include the Simon and Chester graphic novel series and picture books
like *Sir Simon: Super Scarer*, *Where Oliver Fits*, *Monsters 101* and
Unicorns 101 to name a few. Cale has never haunted a potato.

Library and Archives Canada
Cataloguing in Publication

Title: Sir Simon : super scarer
/ Cale Atkinson.

Names: Atkinson, Cale, author,
illustrator.

Description: Previously published: 2018.

Identifiers: Canadiana 20210363630 |
ISBN 9781774880395 (softcover)

Classification:
LCC PS8601.T547 S57 2022 |
DDC jC813/.6 dc23

Library of Congress
Control Number:
2017951214

Published
simultaneously in the
United States of America
by Tundra Books of
Northern New York, an
imprint of Penguin
Random House Canada
Young Readers, a division
of Penguin Random House
of Canada Limited

Edited by Samantha Swenson
The artwork in this book was created with Ghost toots and Photoshop.
The text was set in Tox Typewriter.
Printed in China

1 2 3 4 5   26 25 24 23 22

Penguin
Random House
TUNDRA BOOKS

www.penguinrandomhouse.ca

DEDICATED TO

PA

MA

Have you ever seen a Ghost?

OK, I don't want to freak you out or anything, but . . .

It's OK to be scared. Scaring's what I do.
I'm a professional, you guys.

Check out my business card.

Sir Simon
Super Scarer
Ghostest with the mostest

I've haunted and scared all sorts of things.

I haunted a forest once.

Do you know how hard it is to scare a bear?

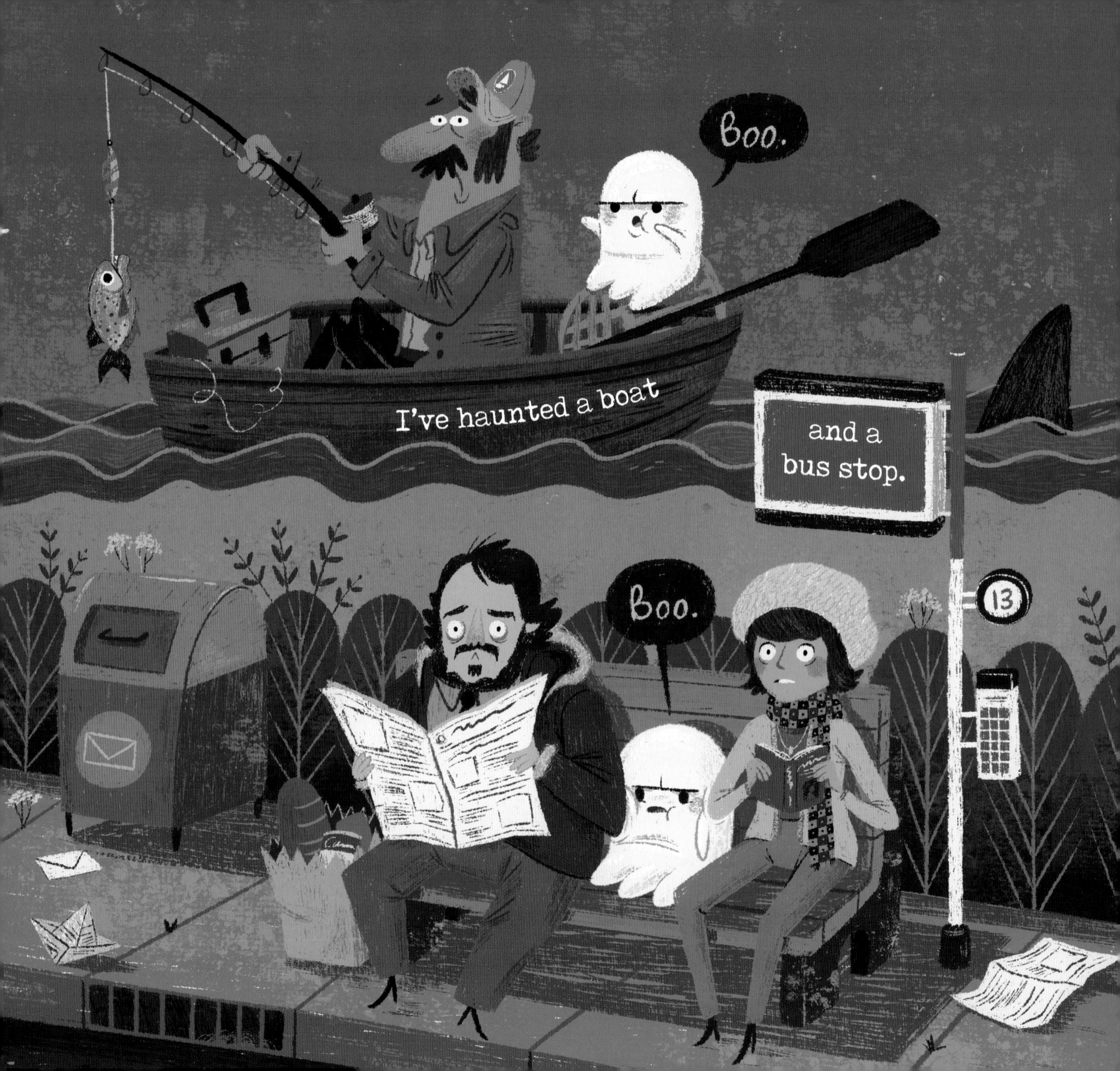
Boo.
I've haunted a boat
and a
bus stop.
Boo.
13

Things I bet you didn't even know COULD be haunted.

The good news is I'm being transferred to a house. My first haunted house!

The bad news is a haunted house
calls for more Ghost chores.
Oh, you don't know what Ghost chores are?
Well, let me tell you, they're the worst.

1:15 a.m.

Stomping
in the attic

STOMP!

1:55 a.m.

Flushing
the toilets

2:10 a.m.

Hiding and moving
things around

3:00 a.m.

Standing creepy in
the window wearing
old-timey clothes

Once I finish my chores, I can get back to doing what I WANT to do.

You don't think I just float around saying BOO all the time, do you? Borrrring!

I have a life outside of being a Ghost, you know! Well, afterlife.

I'm into a bunch of things.

Anyway, here's the best part about this gig:
Rumor has it that grandparents are moving into my house!

THE PYRAMID OF HAUNTING

OLD PEOPLE
PRO: Sleep all the time
CON: None!

BABIES
PRO: Cute-ish
CON: Loud & fart a lot

TEENAGERS
PRO: Totally distracted
CON: Boring

ADULTS
PRO: Mostly too busy to see us
CON: Awake late at night

KIDS
PRO: None!
CON: Too curious

PRE-TEENS
PRO: Easy to scare
CON: Very nosy

In the pyramid of haunting, old people are tops.

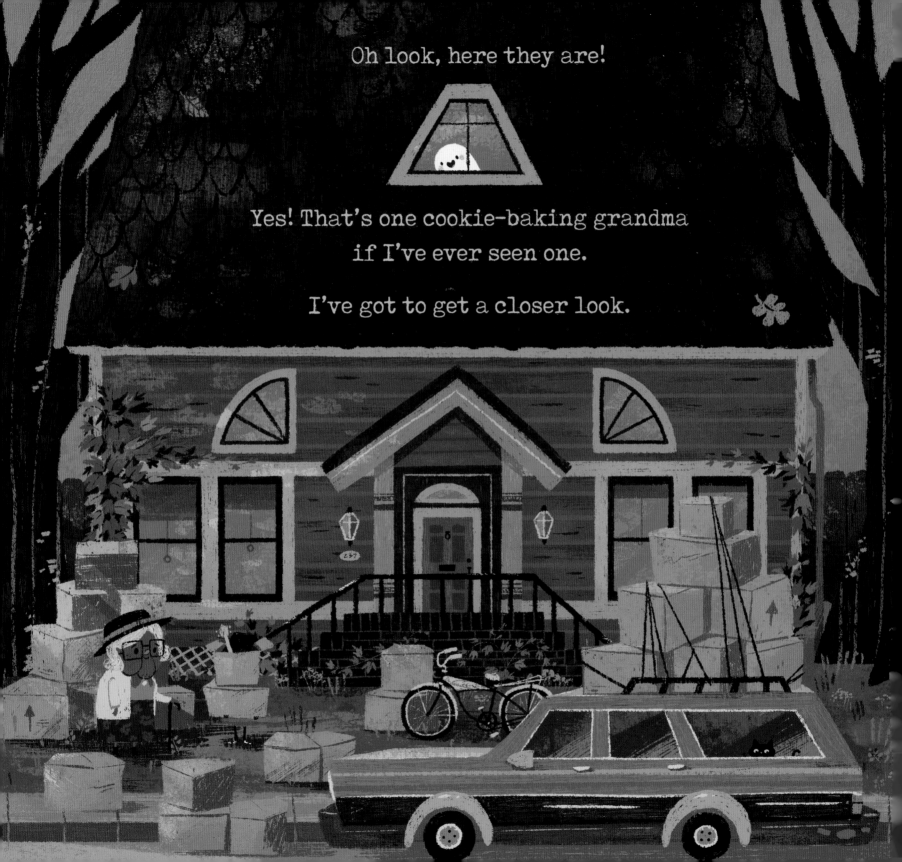

Oh look, here they are!

Yes! That's one cookie-baking grandma
if I've ever seen one.

I've got to get a closer look.

Wow, a real ghost!
I'm Chester, I just moved here with my grandma.
Can you fly
Do you eat ghost food?

I knew ghosts were real!
My grandma said it was all my imagination.

It must be so fun to float around scaring cats and monsters!

Do you sleep in a coffin?

through walls?

Hey, Ghost, can I be a ghost with you?

OK, first of all, don't call me 'Ghost.' It's Simon or Sir Simon Spookington.

Secondly, Chedder—

It's Chester.

I don't have time to play Ghost with you. I've got a ton of chores to get done, and no one else is going to do them for...

waaaait a minute...

Cool, is this your Ghost space?
Don't touch anything!
Neat pictures!
Hey, put that down!

I mean, he wanted to be a Ghost!
If anything, I should be given a medal.

The award for most generous Ghost.
Simon the generous.

What?!
Stop looking at
me like that!

FINE!
I feel bad,
OKAY?

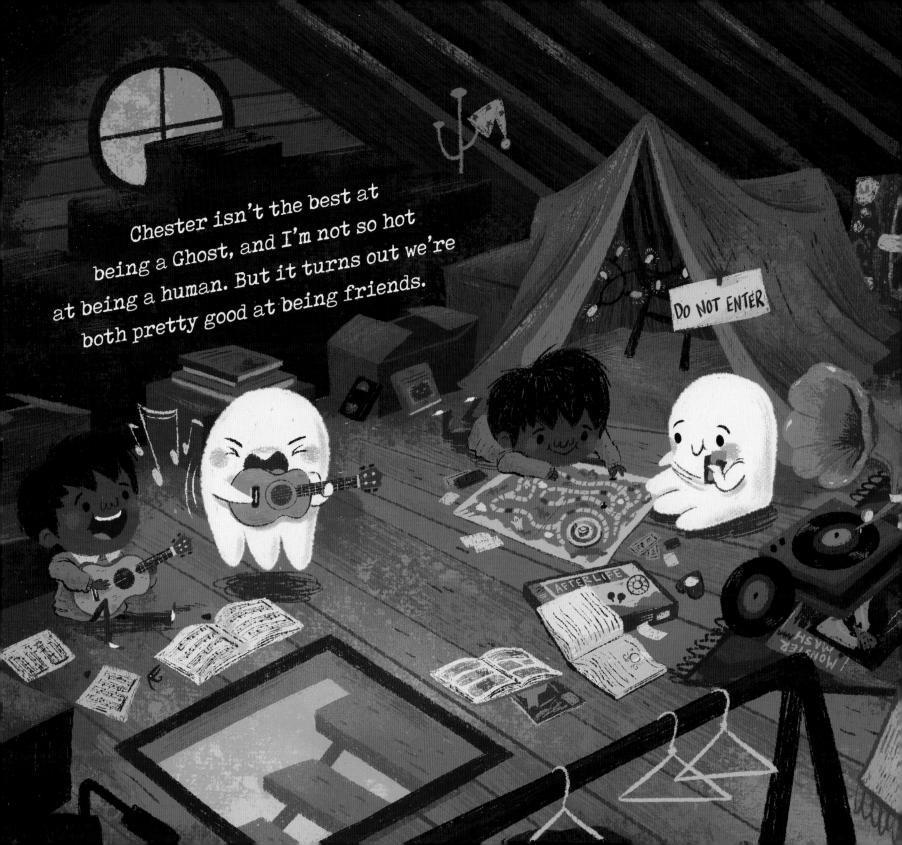

Chester isn't the best at being a Ghost, and I'm not so hot at being a human. But it turns out we're both pretty good at being friends.